Dinorific™ Poetry

Volume 1

*Stories of
ancient animals
created by
a father and son*

Written by Michael Sgrignoli
Ilustrated by Ethan Sgrignoli

Dinorific Poetry Volume 1

FIRST SUNBURY PRESS EDITION
Printed in the United States of America
June 2013

ISBN 978-1-62006-234-0

Library of Congress Control Number: 2010900733

Published by:
Sunbury Press, Inc.
50-A West Main St.
Mechanicsburg, PA   17055

www.sunburypress.com

Mechanicsburg, Pennsylvania   USA

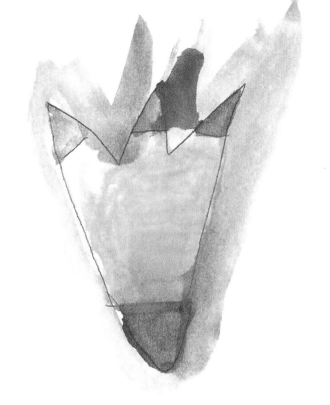

"Dinosaurs may be extinct from the face of the planet, but they are alive and well in our imaginations."
Steve Miller, *FREAKS!*

Backyard Dig

My little boy was pretty sure
    that he would find a dinosaur.
He thought it wouldn't be too hard;
    He started searching our backyard.

He dug in dirt and carved out rocks.
    He dressed in shorts and heavy socks.
And though the beast was long since gone,
    he felt it slept beneath our lawn.

He started digging with a spade.
    He toiled in the late day shade
to find a bone that told the story
    of when the dinos roamed in glory.

So every day, right after school,
    he grabbed his handy digging tool
and boldly strode out to "the dig"
    to search for bones both small and big.

Ethan, age 6

And then one day his shovel scraped
    across a rock – peculiar shape.
He didn't know quite what he'd found.
    He coaxed the relic from the ground.

And there it was – one precious bone!
    He hoped it wasn't there alone.
Most every day another bone
    was freed from rock behind our home.

One single tooth could be enough
    to tell if this chap had the stuff
to stalk and catch his luckless prey.
    A **"carnivore"** is what we'd say.

But as he dug he came to see
    these bones could never ever be
a flesh eater or beastie fierce.
    It hardly had the teeth to pierce.

carnivore (CARN-ih-vore)

Ethan, age 7

It much preferred to have for lunch
    some luscious plants on which to munch.
It lived in herds to thus protect
    the younger ones that foes detect.

This dinosaur lived long ago,
    before we had that lawn to mow.
Before our house and neighborhood
    was built from bricks, cement and wood.

Before there was a street at all
    the dinos lived, and then would fall.
And what are left are bones to tell
    just when and where the dinos fell.

Ethan, age 7

These bones that slowly turned to stone
      remind us that we're not alone.
This world was once a steamy place,
      so long before the human race.

And this is why my boy did search
      amongst the oak, the pine…the birch.
Behind our shed he found his quest.
      Not even taking one day's rest.

He knew it'd be no easy task.
      And as for help? He never asked.
And though the ground was not so porous
      my boy unearthed a **STEGOSAURUS**!

Stegosaurus (steg-oh-SORE-us)

Stegosaurus
Ethan, age 7

My Giant Friend, Diplodocus

He'd never fit his body through
    the swing-out door like me and you.
And so he'd never ride our bus --
    my giant friend, **DIPLODOCUS**.

He'd walk to school, instead, to learn
    the subjects that are our concern.
Of course he might chew chalk to dust --
    my hungry friend, Diplodocus.

Geology and History --
    sometimes they can be tough for me.
He'd prob'ly earn an A + + --
    my learned friend, Diplodocus.

Diplodocus (di-PLAWD-ih-cuss)

He'd graduate in five months flat --
    He wouldn't boast. I'll tell you that.
He'd leave top students in the dust --
    my humble friend, Diplodocus.

And then next year he would return.
    And it would be our turn to learn
from he who'd traveled our Earth's crust --
    my worldly friend, Diplodocus.

Do you suppose that he could teach
    from books that may be hard to reach?
In truth, it's never been discussed --
    my long-necked friend, Diplodocus.

And at day's end, I'd ride him home.
    We'd startle people as we'd roam.
But have no fear, it's only just...
    my closest friend, Diplodocus.

Diplodocus
Ethan, age 7

The Dimetrodon's Tale

DIMETRODON had a tall sail on his back.
  Don't know if its color was red, green or black.
This back sail stood straight up – it never would fold.
  It must have been quite a cool sight to behold.

It probably helped him a lot when the sun
  rose up in the morn' and his sleeping was done.
He needed to warm up and go find some food.
  As predators go, he was one hungry dude!

It could have been there to avoid an attack
  from other big meat-eaters out for a snack.
Perhaps it was meant to attract a new mate.
  Whatever it was, we can just speculate.

This fellow had two different teeth in his jaw --
  The one kind could stab and the other could gnaw.
So we can construe he chewed food for his gizzard,
  which makes him quite different than your normal lizard.

Dimetrodon (di-MET-trah-don)

A lizard can only take bites and then swallow.
    They gulp one chunk down and another would follow.
Dimetrodon's teeth put all lizards to shame --
    another key fact that has lead to his fame.

He grew to eleven feet long, we surmise.
    His bones tell the story of stature and size.
And scientists think he weighed 500 pounds.
    We just have to guess if he ever made sounds.

But when you dig deeper and learn a bit more,
    you find that he's not a true blue dinosaur.
He really should be classified as a mammal --
    which makes him linked closer to aardvark and camel.

This creature lived long before dinosaurs did.
    A noteworthy fact about such I don't kid.
He once ruled this land with his 3-foot-high sail.
    And now you all know the Dimetrodon's tale.

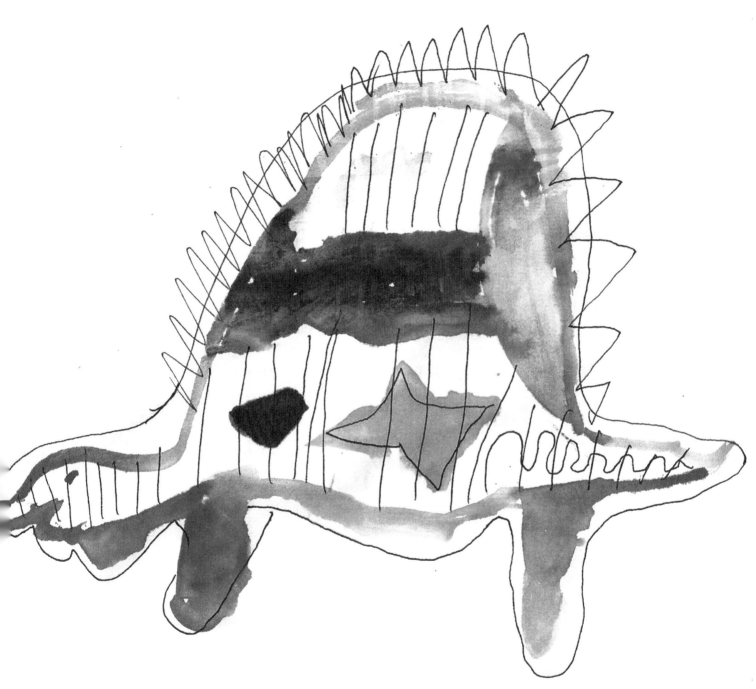

Dimetrodon
Ethan, age 8

A Trip To The Museum

Walk down this long hall to the dinosaur room
and take note what these creatures liked to consume.

Some grazed on high tree tops and plants by the score.
So as a result we say they're "**herbivore**."

Some dinosaurs never touched veggies, just meat.
The term "**carnivore**" explains what they would eat.

And then there were "**omnivores**." Here's what they'd chew
some meat and some plants. Frankly either would do.

herbivore (URR-bih-vore)

carnivore (CARN-ih-vore)

omnivores (AHM-nih-vores)

Ethan, age 7

And now 'round this corner…the reason we came.
Let's try to identify all here by name.

Huge powerful jawbone and leg muscles flex.
You're first to encounter the mighty T-Rex.

A long-crested head that's much bigger than all of us.
Step up and look closely at **PARASAUROLOPHUS**.

That club on his tail could sure make you feel sore.
It's none other than a big **ANKYLOSAUR**!

One look at his thumb spikes and I'd sure move on.
This beast, he is known as an **IGUANODON**.

Parasaurolophus (PARE-uh-sore-RAH-luh-fuss)

Ankylosaur (ann-KI-lo-sore)

Iguanodon (ee-GWON-oh-don)

Iguanodon
Ethan, age 7

A 20-foot ostrich? That'd sure cause a fuss.
Let's all learn together. It's **GALLIMIMUS**.

Tail feathers. Sharp teeth. Toes that numbered to six.
He's 3 feet of terror named **CAUDIPTERYX**.

If we walked on by, I hope he would ignore us --
the largest known flesh-eater, **GIGANOTOSAURUS**.

She's 16 feet wide, nearly 14 feet long!
That's one giant turtle: the great **ARCHELON**.

Gallimimus (gah-lee-MI-muss)

Caudipteryx (cow-DIP-ter-ix)

Giganotosaurus (JIG-uh-note-a-SORE-us)

Archelon (ARR-kee-lohn)

Archelon
Ethan, age 7

A group of these beasts were caught up in some crisis.
That's why we know so much about COELOPHYSIS.

And now that our day viewing dinos is done,
let's head for the car. The hard rain makes us run.

We can't wait to come back and spend some more time
researching these creatures and making a rhyme.

We're sure, when we do, they'll be more poems to read.
Our imaginations are easy to feed.

Coelophysis (see-lo-FI-sis)

Coelophysis
Ethan, age 7

Plesiosaur

Now let me introduce you to a **PLESIOSAUR**.
   The most intriguing swimming gal you'll find, I'm sure.
She's got a lovely neck that looks much like a snake;
   a body that is rounded like a turtle's shape.

We think she'd grow to 40 feet or even more.
   We reason that she'd rarely ever come ashore.
So did she struggle out to lay her eggs on land?
   More likely she stayed in the sea avoiding sand.

T'was many years ago her fossil'd bones were found
   and eager scientists did free her bones from ground.
For they were on a hunt the likes we'd never seen --
   a quest of Edward Drinker Cope, a lifelong dream.

Plesiosaur (PLEE-zee-uh-sore)

When they'd unearth her bones, to Mr. Cope they'd send.
      But he attached her skull to the complete wrong end.
And later on they figured out the neck was long
      and placing skulls atop tail bones was just plain wrong.

Some say she is the fabled monster from Loch Ness.
      It sure would be a thrill to know her true address –
but up until today it's little more than spoof.
      So legends will continue since there's no real proof.

And here's one final fact about this plesiosaur:
      we've found a lot of pebbles in her belly stored.
She must have kept them there to help her food digest.
      or make it easier for her to swim, we've guessed.

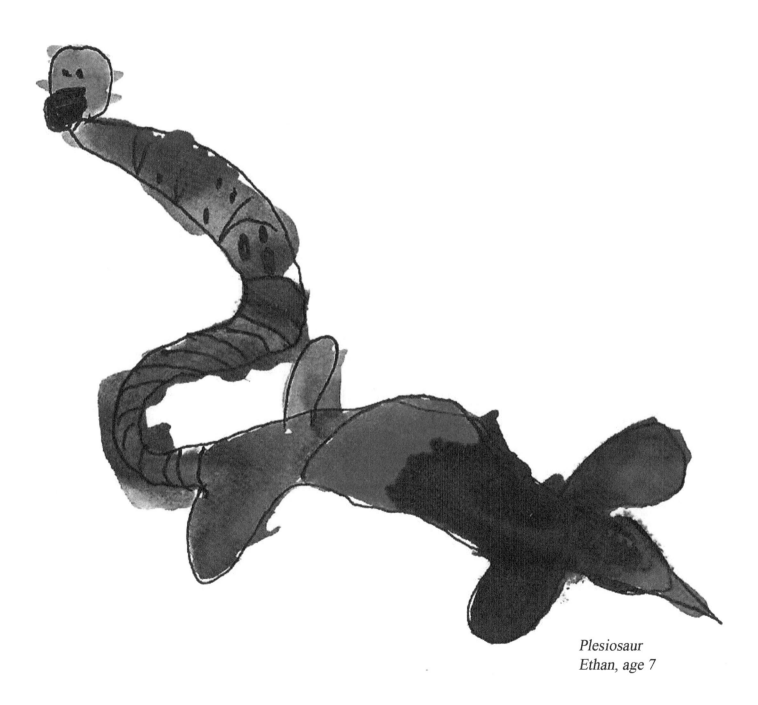

Plesiosaur
Ethan, age 7

Wacky Pachycephalosaur

Wacky **PACHYCEPHALOSAUR** --
    tell me, does your head get sore?
Ramming it against your pal,
    trying to impress some gal.
Wacky Pachycephalosaur --
    late at night we hear you snore.
You're exhausted from your fight --
    crashing heads all day and night.
Wacky Pachycephalosaur --
    here's one brute that's not a bore!
Bash and bam – the sound is great.
    Smashing with his hard head plate.
Wacky Pachycephalosaur--
    scientists are not so sure.
Did you really use that dome
    to protect your mate and home?
Wacky Pachycephalosaur --
    every theory yields ten more.
Maybe you decided that
    it's a great place for a hat.

Pachycephalosaur (pack-ee-SEFF-uh-lo-SORE)

Pachycephalosaurus
Ethan, age 7

Do You Suppose?

Do you suppose **STYRACOSAURUS**
    ever sang a song?
And, if she did, would you suppose
    it lasted all day long?

You sort of have to figure that
    it must've been quite loud.
You have to then assume, of course,
    that it would draw a crowd.

Styracosaurus (sty-RACK-uh-SORE-us)

Styracosaurus
Ethan, age 8

What if an **ALLOSAURUS** learned
     to play a bass guitar?
For goodness sake I'm sure that folks
     would come from near and far.

The rumble of those bottom notes
     would really shake the Earth.
About as much as when he jumped
     and ground withstood his girth.

Allosaurus (al-uh-SORE-us)

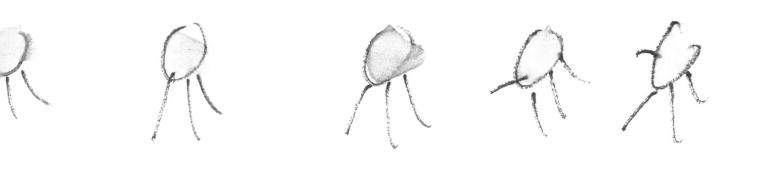

Allosaurus
Ethan, age 8

Perhaps T-Rex would play guitar
   and he'd be well in charge.
He'd have to play one normal-sized,
   his arms weren't very large.

He'd have a knack for harmonies
   and sometimes he'd sing lead.
He'd learn it all by listening --
   no music could he read.

Tyrannosaurus Rex
Ethan, age 8

I bet **IGUANODON** had loads
    of talent in his thumbs.
And when he'd try, he'd soon find out
    that he could play the drums.

He'd practice night and day to hit
    the toms, the kick, the snare.
He'd flick his tail and send his cymbals
    sailing through the air.

Iguanodon (ee-GWON-uh-don)

Iguanodon
Ethan, age 8

I see a beast a-pounding on
     a keyboard made of stone.
It's just **AMARGASAURUS**.
          On piano she's well-known.

She's quite the flashy player;
     she would sway from side to side
and strike the keys with her back spikes
     while grinning really wide.

Amargasaurus (uh-MAR-guh-SORE-us)

Amargasaurus
Ethan, age 8

They'd call themselves "The Really,
    Really Old Kids on the Block."
And man, I gotta tell ya,
    for old fossils, they would rock!

They'd learn some songs and for their fans
    they'd play a local venue.
They'd look for places that had meats
    and plants both on the menu.

Their fans – they all would concentrate
    and memorize each sound.
They had no choice, of course, because
    iPods were not around.

So there's the band, a wild group
    that's ready for the stage.
I'll have to tell you more sometime --
    but that's another page.

MEAT THE R.R.O.K. ON THE BLOCK!
The First Album by Pangaea's Phenomenal Pop Combo

"Guanny"

REALLY
REALLY

"Big Al"

OLD
KIDS

"Sty"

ON
THE

"Rex"

BLOCK

"Margo"

The Fossil

There were many dinosaurs
    that you could say were docile.
Thankfully a lot of them
    were turned into a fossil.

Studying these rocks can give
    us loads of information.
All about the dinosaurs
    and even Earth's creation.

Now we know some dinosaurs
    had lovely feathers sprouting.
Years ago some scientists
    were skeptical and doubting.

Every day discoveries
    are made that keep us learning –
helping us to answer all
    those questions that were burning.

Ethan, age 7

Evidence from fossils says
    a meteor came crashing.
YUCATAN PENINSULA
    is where it did the smashing.

People thought that this was surely
    why most life was ended.
Sunlight was obscured and on
    it most of Earth depended.

Did it cause the dinosaurs to vanish?
    Some don't buy it.
Now another theory claims
    volcanoes changed the climate.

Where should we be looking for
    a theory that's colossal?
Right back where we started from
    ...the all-important fossil.

Yucatan Peninsula (YOO-cuh-tan pen-IN-soo-luh)

Ethan, age 7

Nigersaurus

Now here would be a handy guy
    to have when things were spilled.
The clever **NIGERSAURUS** was
    a tame one and quite skilled.

He had a mouth that had a shape
    more handy than a broom.
In fact it was exactly in
    the shape of a vacuum.

And here's the thing where even a
    new vacuum can't compete.
He had a set of grinding teeth
    that helped when he would eat.

Imagine if your vacuum sucked
    your mess up off the floor --
then grinded it and mashed it up
    so it could suck some more.

Nigersaurus (NEE-jur-SORE-us)

And even if he lost a tooth
    while vacuuming the ground,
existing right behind it was
    more rows of teeth, we've found.

Just like a shark, when one fell out,
    a new tooth took its place.
The mighty Nigersaurus had
    a most amazing face.

A Dr. Paul Sereno
    excavated him and learns
this ancient cow kept his head low
    to nibble on the ferns.

Another bone's discovery
    has helped us understand.
There's countless more awaiting
    under hardened rock and sand.

Each year we learn a little more
    than those that came before us:
like ancient cows with vacuum mouths --
    the gentle nigersaurus.

Nigersaurus
Ethan, age 9

Sleep Tight, Triceratops

Sleep tight my young **TRICERATOPS**.
    You had a big, big day.
Tomorrow there'll be more to do
    and many games to play.

Tomorrow is approaching fast --
    the school bus won't be late.
You'll learn new things throughout the day
    and at the stop I'll wait.

I'll meet you close to 4 o'clock
    and we'll jump in the car.
And off to Hummelstown we'll go --
    it's really not so far.

I know a store that's filled with things
    you'll love to hunt and find.
One hundred dinosaurs to view
    brought there by Mr. Stine.

Triceratops (tri-SARE-uh-tops)

Triceratops
Ethan, age 7

So many dinosaurs are there,
  it's awfully hard to choose.
And then there are the many
  different mammals to peruse.

Tomorrow after school we'll go
  and at those toys we'll stare.
No matter what you're looking for
  it's at Toys On The Square.

So it's all set, Triceratops.
  Let sleepy eyes now close.
I'll tuck you in and keep you warm --
  your shoulders, hands and toes.

Now rest my young Triceratops;
  like **PTEROSAURS** you'll fly.
And in your dreams you'll soar to heights
  to touch the blue, blue sky.

Pterosaurs (TARE-uh-sores)

Pterosaur
Ethan, age 7

If you enjoyed this book as much as we loved creating it,
check these out:

Dinorific Poetry, Volume 2

Dinorific Poetry, Volume 3

Tell us which poems and pictures are your favorite:
www.dinorhymes.com

To schedule an author/artist visit or presentation,
contact us at: sales@dinorhymes.com

Have a favorite dinosaur picture of your own?
Send us a copy for consideration in a future volume!

CPSIA information can be obtained at www.ICGtesting.com
Printed in the USA
BVOW10s2205101213

338760BV00002B/7/P